A Note to Parents and Caregivers:

Read-it! Joke Books are for children who are moving ahead on the amazing road to reading. These fun books support the acquisition and extension of reading skills as well as a love of books.

Published by the same company that produces *Read-it!* Readers, these books introduce the question/answer and dialogue patterns that help children expand their thinking about language structure and book formats.

When sharing joke books with a child, read in short stretches. Pause often to talk about the meaning of the jokes. The question/answer and dialogue formats work well for this purpose and provide an opportunity to talk about the language and meaning of the jokes. Have the child turn the pages and point to the pictures and familiar words. When you read the jokes, have fun creating the voices of characters or emphasizing some important words. Be sure to reread favorite jokes.

There is no right or wrong way to share books with children. Find time to read with your child, and pass on the legacy of literacy.

Adria F. Klein, Ph.D.
Professor Emeritus
California State University
San Bernardino, California

Editor: Christianne Jones
Designer: Joe Anderson
Page Production: Melissa Kes
Art Director: Keith Griffin
Managing Editor: Catherine Neitge
The illustrations in this book were prepared digitally.

Picture Window Books
5115 Excelsior Boulevard
Suite 232
Minneapolis, MN 55416
877-845-8392
www.picturewindowbooks.com

Printed in the United States of America.

Library of Congress Cataloging-in-Publication Data
Ziegler, Mark, 1954-
Goofballs! : a book of sports jokes / written by Mark Ziegler ;
illustrated by Anne Haberstroh.
p. cm. — (Read-it! joke books—supercharged!)
ISBN 1-4048-0965-1
1. Sports—Juvenile humor. 2. Riddles, Juvenile. I. Haberstroh, Anne.
II. Title. III. Series.

PN6231.S65Z54 2004
818'.602—dc22   2004018443

Goofballs!
A Book of Sports Jokes

By Mark Ziegler • Illustrated by Anne Haberstroh

Reading Advisers:

Adria F. Klein, Ph.D.
Professor Emeritus, California State University
San Bernardino, California

Susan Kesselring, M.A., Literacy Educator
Rosemount-Apple Valley-Eagan (Minnesota) School District

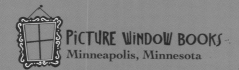
PICTURE WINDOW BOOKS
Minneapolis, Minnesota

What kind of hair do surfers have?

Wavey.

Why was Cinderella such a bad soccer player?

Because she always ran away from the ball.

Why wouldn't they let the baby play basketball?

She wouldn't stop dribbling.

Why did the bowling pins refuse to stand up?

They were on strike.

What do you call a basketball player's pet parrot?

A personal fowl.

Why did the chicken join the cheerleading squad?

She liked to egg on the team.

What color is a hockey score?

Goaled.

What's the hardest thing about skydiving?

The ground.

Why did the golfer always wear two pairs of pants?

In case he got a hole in one.

Why did the kangaroo lose the basketball game?

He ran out of bounds.

Why is a soccer stadium the coolest place in the world?

Because it's full of fans.

What does a runner lose when he wins a race?

His breath.

What do you call your dad when he water-skis in the winter?

A Popsicle.

What is the quietest sport to play?

Bowling. You can hear a pin drop.

Why did the football coach rip apart the pay telephone?

He was trying to get his quarter back.

What dessert should a basketball player never eat?

Turnovers.

What are two things a skateboarder will never eat for breakfast?

Lunch and dinner.

What is the noisiest sport in the world?

Tennis. Players always raise a racket on the court.

How can you tell that elephants are crazy about swimming?

They never take off their trunks.

What's the difference between a dog and a basketball player?

One drools and one dribbles.

Why did the tennis player always carry a flashlight?

Because he lost all his matches.

Where do golfers go after a game?

A tee party.

Why did the frog
try out for the
baseball team?

He liked catching pop flies.

What has wings and a skateboard?

Tony Hawk.

What do you call a girl who's good at
catching hockey pucks?

Annette.

Why should you be careful
playing sports in the jungle?

Because it's full of cheetahs.

Why did the soccer ball
quit the team?

It was tired of getting kicked around.

What do you call a pig that knows karate?

A pork chop.

What is a swimmer's favorite game?

Pool.

Did you hear about the race between the lettuce and the banana?

The lettuce was ahead.

What kind of insect is bad at football?

A fumble bee.

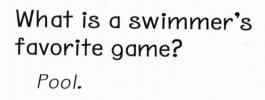

Why did the chicken cross the basketball court?

It heard the referee calling fowls.

Why do artists never win when they play soccer?

The game always ends in a draw.

What football team travels with the most luggage?

The Packers.

What is an electric eel's favorite football team?

The Chargers.

Why did the softball player take her bat to the library?

Her teacher told her
to hit the books.

What's the best thing for joggers to drink?

Running water.

Why do the fastest bowlers
make the most strikes?

They have no time to spare.

Where can you find the largest
diamond in the world?

On a baseball field.

What is the best way to hold
a baseball bat?

By the wings.

**Why did the jogger
look so angry?**

She was a cross-country runner.

**Why didn't the dog want
to play soccer?**

Because he was a boxer.

**Why did the soccer fan bring
a rope to the game?**

So he could tie up the score.

**How is a scrambled egg like
a bad football team?**

They both get beaten.

What did the right soccer shoe
say to the left soccer shoe?

*"Between us, we're gonna
have a ball!"*

Read-it! Joke Books— Supercharged!

Beastly Laughs: A Book of Monster Jokes by Michael Dahl

Chalkboard Chuckles: A Book of Classroom Jokes by Mark Moore

Creepy Crawlers: A Book of Bug Jokes by Mark Moore

Critter Jitters: A Book of Animal Jokes by Mark Ziegler

Giggle Bubbles: A Book of Underwater Jokes by Mark Ziegler

Goofballs! A Book of Sports Jokes by Mark Ziegler

Lunchbox Laughs: A Book of Food Jokes by Mark Ziegler

Roaring with Laughter: A Book of Animal Jokes by Michael Dahl

School Kidders: A Book of School Jokes by Mark Ziegler

Sit! Stay! Laugh! A Book of Pet Jokes by Michael Dahl

Spooky Sillies: A Book of Ghost Jokes by Mark Moore

Wacky Wheelies: A Book of Transportation Jokes by Mark Ziegler

Looking for a specific title or level? A complete list of *Read-it!* Readers is available on our Web site: *www.picturewindowbooks.com*